Happy Birthday, Dear Dragon

A Follett JUST Beginning-To-Read book

Happy Birthday, Dear Dragon

Margaret Hillert

Illustrated by Carl Kock

FOLLETT PUBLISHING COMPANY Chicago

International Standard Book Number: 0-695-40743-0 Library edition

International Standard Book Number: 0-695-30743-6 Paper edition

Fourth Printing

This looks good, Mother.
What a big one.
Oh, this is fun.

Here is something.
What is it?
I can not guess.

Oh, look here.
Look at this
—and this
—and this!

7

And here is something that can jump up.

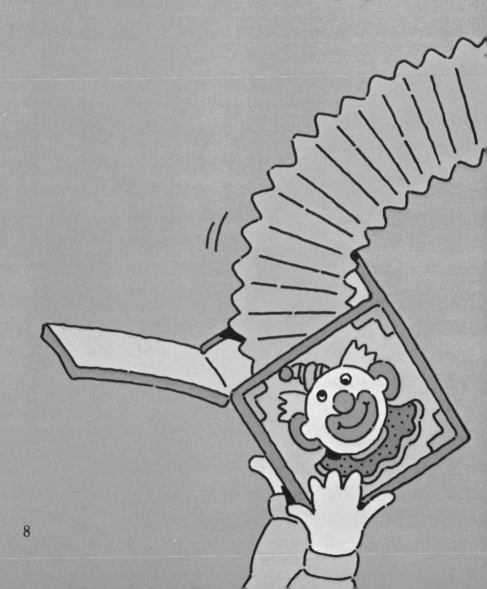

Now come with me.

I want to get you something.

Run, run, run.

Here we go.
In here. In here.
We will look at the dogs.

13

But we have a dog, Father.
I like the one we have.
I do not want this dog.

Here is something little.
Do you want this?
You can look at it.
It can look at you.

No, I do not like it.

What can it do?

It can not play with me.

Look down here.
You can have this one.
Do you like it?
See it jump.

I like that little one.
But it is not what I want.
Come away.
Come away.

Here is what I want.

Oh, will you get it for me?

I like it.

    I like it.

        I like it!

Come with me.
Come to my house.
I like you.
We can have fun.

20

Look, Mother.
See what I have.
It can play with me.

I see. I see.
It is funny.
We will find something for it.

I want to go for a ride.
I will get in.
Help me.
Help me.

Here we go.
Run, run, run.
What fun.
What fun.

25

Will you do something for me?

Will you help me with this?

Now, *you* have one.

Have two.

Have three.

You are a big help.

Oh, my. Oh, my.
Look what you can do.
I like this.

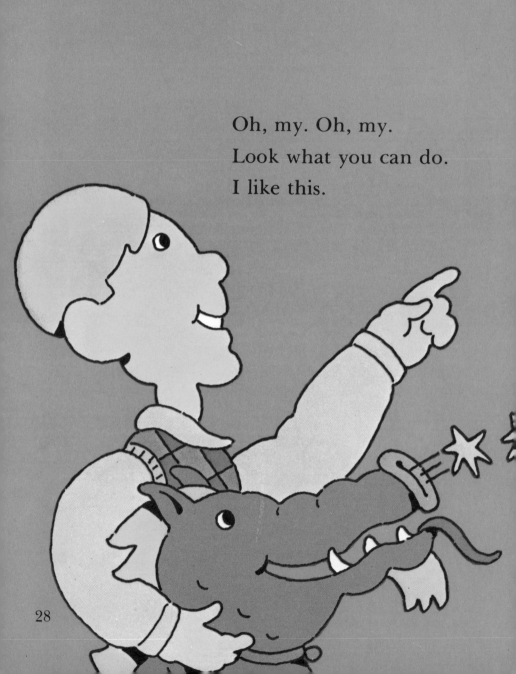

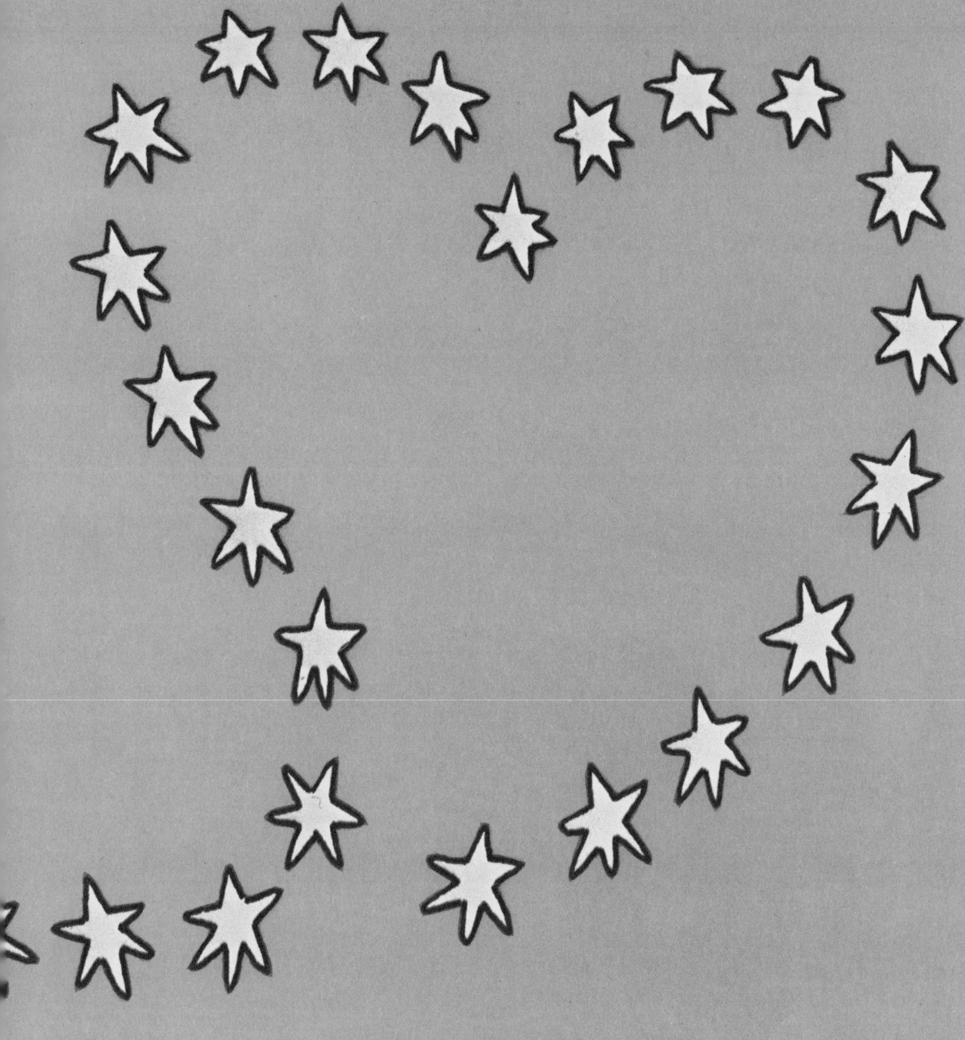

Here you are with me.
And here I am with you.
Oh, what a happy birthday, dear dragon.

Happy Birthday, Dear Dragon

Uses of This Book: Reading for fun. This easy-to-read story about a delightful pet is sure to excite the rich imaginations of children.

Word List

All of the 64 words used in *Happy Birthday, Dear Dragon* are listed. Regular verb forms and plurals of words already on the list are not listed separately, but the endings are given in parentheses after the word.

1	happy		it		you		see
	birthday		I		run	**18**	away
	dear		can	**12**	we	**19**	for
	dragon		not		go	**20**	my
5	this		guess		in		house
	look(s)	**7**	at		will	**23**	funny
	good		and		the		find
	mother	**8**	that		dog(s)	**24**	ride
	what		jump	**14**	but		help
	a		up		have	**27**	two
	big	**10**	now		father		three
	one		come		like		are
	oh		with		do	**31**	am
	is		me	**15**	little		
	fun		want	**16**	no		
6	here		to		play		
	something		get	**17**	down		